This book belongs to

....

This is the story of Samaritan Sam,

Can you read it? Yes, you can!

There's something else. Can you guess what?

On every page there's a mouse to spot

The Good Samaritan

Nick and Claire Page

Illustrations by Nikky Loy

make
believe
ideas

So here's the tale as I heard it.
There's this man, see?
Never done anyone any harm,
always minds his own business.
He's Izzy the Israelite. Is he? Right!
And he needs to get to Jericho, right?
And he lives in Jerusalem, see?

Well, it's a risky old road, that.
From Jerusalem to Jericho.
It's as rough as a rocky riverbed,
as winding as a wiggly worm,
as slippery as a slithery snake.

So anyway, he's walking along, is Izzy,
whistling to stop himself from being afraid.

Time goes by.
One o'clock: he's OK.
Two o'clock: on his way.
Three o'clock: it's a nice day –
blue skies above, sun shining down,
and only the rocks for shade.

Suddenly Izzy the Israelite notices
a flicker in the shadows.
Izzy's not alone. Is he? No.
There are thieves in the thickets,
robbers in the rocks,
bandits behind the boulders.

Robbers rush at him.
BIP! BAP! BOUF!
Thieves thump him.
OW! OUCH! OOF!
Bandits bash him and beat him up badly.
They take all his money, dump him in
a ditch and run away.

He's dizzy, is Izzy.
Is he? Very.
Perhaps someone will
walk by and help him.

Time goes by.
Four o'clock: no one near.
Five o'clock: sheds a tear.
Six o'clock: someone's here!

Here comes Parish the priest.

"He's holy! He'll help," says Izzy to himself.
Parish the priest sees Izzy lying by the side
of the road. And he crosses over to the other
side and keeps on walking!

I ask you! Is that properly priestly?
Is that godly and good? No.

Time goes by.
Seven o'clock: still no news.
Eight o'clock: badly bruised.
Nine o'clock: the sound of shoes.

Here comes Harris the temple helper.
"He's holy! He'll help," says Izzy to himself.
Harris the helper sees Izzy lying by the
side of the road. And he crosses over to
the other side and keeps on walking!
I ask you! Is that helpfully holy?
Is that godly and good? No.

Time goes by.
Ten o'clock: no light.
Eleven o'clock: what a fright!
Twelve o'clock: midnight.
Then along the road comes
Sam the Samaritan.
"He's horrible. He won't help,"
says Izzy to himself.

Now, as you know, Samaritans and Israelites,
they don't get along.
They fight like cats and dogs,
like lions and bears,
like... Israelites and Samaritans.
They're always arguing and forever fighting.

Would someone from Samaria
help someone from Israel?
What would you say?
Would someone from Israel
help someone from Samaria?
No way.

But when Sam the Samaritan sees
Izzy the Israelite lying by the side
of the road, he stops.
He steps over.
He stoops down to have a closer look.

Then Sam the Samaritan picks Izzy up and
washes out his wounds,
bandages his bruises,
cleans up his cuts.

Then he takes Izzy to a nearby inn
where he nurses him through the night
to the new day.
I ask you! Is that helpfully holy?
Is that godly and good? Yes!

And the next morning, Sam, he says to
the innkeeper, "Here is some money to look
after Izzy. If he needs anything more,
give him the goods,
add it to my bill,
I'll repay you when I return."
Then he goes on his way.

RECEPTION

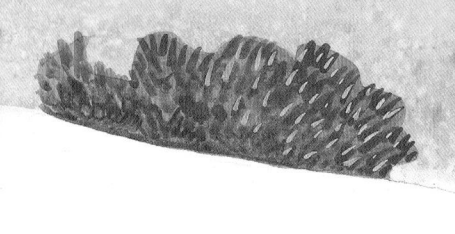

And that's the tale as I heard it.
Now I ask you this.
Who showed lots of love?
Who scored the highest in holiness?
Who was godly and good?
Not Parish the priest;
Not Harris the temple helper;
But Sam, the very, very
good Samaritan.

Ready to tell

Oh no! Some of the pictures from this story have been mixed up! Can you retell the story and point to each picture in the correct order?

RECEPTION

Picture dictionary

Encourage your child to read these harder words from the story and gradually develop their basic vocabulary.

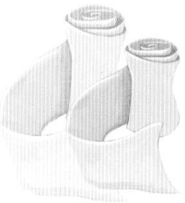

bandage

boulders

donkey

money

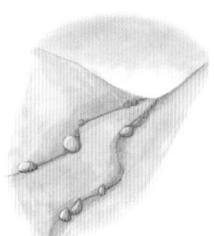

road

robbers

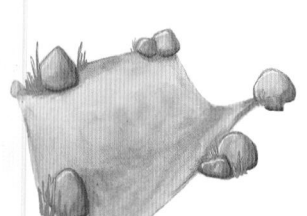

rocks

thicket

walking

Key words

Here are some key words used in context. Help your child to use other words from the border in simple sentences.

Izzy was walking **to** Jericho.

"**We** will rob him," they said.

"Please help **me**," Izzy cried.

The priest walked **away**.

This man helped Izzy.

Wicked wounds!

If you're play acting and want to pretend that you've been in a fight, like Izzy, here are some useful tips.

You will need

1 tbs petroleum jelly • a pinch of cocoa powder • red and blue food coloring • a bowl • facial tissues

What to do

1 Place petroleum jelly in a bowl.

2 Add a drop of food coloring (red and blue) and mix. Stir in the cocoa powder to make a dark blood color.

3 Separate a tissue. Using one layer, tear the tissue into a small rectangle and place on the wound site.

4 Cover the tissue with petroleum jelly and mold into the shape of a wound with a dip in the middle.

5 Fill the middle with the petroleum jelly mixture.

Other gruesome ideas

You can make fake, runny blood by mixing red and blue food coloring with a little clear honey and a drop or two of liquid soap.

Use yellow, brown, purple, and blue eyeshadow and blush to create convincing bruises.

Take care: Food coloring may stain clothing or fabric. Use soap and warm water to wash off the makeup.

Ainsi va la vie

Max n'a
per

Dominique de Saint Mars

Serge Bloch

© CALLIGRAM

CHRISTIAN ○ ALLIMARD

**T'es vraiment nul !
Tu vas nous faire
perdre !**

**Laisse, Max, c'est pas
sa faute... T'avais qu'à
défendre mieux !**

6

7

CHEZ LUI, MAX A TOUT RACONTÉ...

Tu n'étais pas assez concentré! Tu te rattraperas au match de tennis!

Ne t'en fais pas. L'important, ce n'est pas de gagner, mais de participer*!

* Phrase de Pierre de Coubertin, créateur des Jeux olympiques modernes en 1896.

10

Ça se voit que tu ne sais pas ce que c'est de perdre !
C'est pas grave... Il faut bien que quelqu'un gagne et que quelqu'un perde, c'est le jeu !

Évidemment, toi, t'es nulle en sport, alors tu ne peux même pas avoir envie de gagner !
Pauvre type !

13

14

Mais Max... Tes pieds sur le canapé !

Et voilà !

VOUS M'AVEZ FAIT PERDRE !!! JE SUIS DÉGOÛTÉ... J'ALLAIS GAGNER !

Mais reviens, Max, on va faire un Zig Zag !

Qu'est-ce qui se passe avec Max? Il vient de sortir de la maison en pleurant...

Il a perdu... Il en fait encore une tragédie.

Venez, on va le chercher...

18

19

Mais je t'assure que j'aurais gagné si vous ne m'aviez pas...

Ah ! NON. Tu ne vas pas recommencer !

Bon... Mais, après ça, on dit que je suis nul...

21

22

Max, le mammifère qu'on appelle la plus belle conquête de l'homme, c'est : la vache, la poule ou le chev...?

Fastoooooche ! C'est la vache !

Mais non, c'est le cheval !

AH, AH! ... Remarque, si tu lui enlèves ses cornes, à ta vache.

OH, OH, OH!

AH, AH!

C'est ce que je voulais dire, le cheval. Évidemment!

Moi, j'arrête, vous me faites perdre exprès! Ou bien j'ai le droit de rejouer.

Ah! NON.

Tu peux accepter de rater une question! Tu ne vas pas en mourir!

Allez rigole, Max !
Et on dit : « Malheureux
au jeu, heureux en
amour ! »

Mais qu'est-ce qu'il y a
encore, mon lapin ?

Il ne supporte
pas de perdre, Max !
Il est trop orgueilleux.

29

31

Jeu Alexis, qui mène 5 à 2!

YEAH!

Elle était faute, la balle !

Silence, s'il vous plaît.

Max gagne le jeu. Alexis mène 5 jeux à 3.

De toute façon, je suis fier de t'avoir comme fils !

Mais qu'est-ce qu'il lui prend? Il a perdu trois jeux! Ah, enfin, il joue mieux!

Zut, là, ça va mal.

Balle de match...

FAUTE!

Non, je crois que sa balle était bonne... Il peut la rejouer.

37

Bravo, mon Max!

Tu as été beau joueur. Il y a des défaites dont on sort gagnant...

La prochaine fois, je te parie que tu gagnes.

Un pari comme ça, je veux bien le perdre!

Et toi…

Est-ce qu'il t'est arrivé la même histoire qu'à Max?
Réponds aux deux questionnaires…

Trouves-tu que ce n'est pas la peine de jouer si ce n'est pas pour gagner? As-tu déjà triché ou menti pour gagner?

Es-tu malheureux et déçu par toi-même si tu perds? Te sens-tu soudain nul en tout? Oublies-tu ce que tu réussis?

As-tu peur qu'on se moque de toi si tu perds? Es-tu jaloux de ceux qui t'ont battu?

As-tu peur de décevoir quelqu'un que tu aimes
ou que tu admires? et que l'on t'aime moins?

Quand tu as perdu, te mets-tu en colère? Boudes-tu
sans rien dire? ou trouves-tu de mauvaises excuses?

Est-ce que tu traites facilement les autres de mauvais
joueurs? Ça t'énerve qu'on te dise la même chose?

Penses-tu que l'on puisse être très motivé pour gagner,
et quand même accepter de perdre?

Aimes-tu surtout t'amuser et t'améliorer
sans te demander qui est le meilleur ou le plus fort?

Comprends-tu que pour tes parents, ce n'est pas grave
que tu perdes? Te sens-tu aimé de toute façon?

Je gagnerai la prochaine fois ou la prochaine prochaine...

Perds-tu souvent? Es-tu triste ou penses-tu à ce que tu as déjà réussi et que tu gagneras la prochaine fois?

Allez, souris !

Connais-tu des gens qui sont prêts à tout pour gagner? Arrives-tu à être ami avec eux? à les faire sourire?

Vive le jeu !

C'est du sport !

Ce qui est génial dans le jeu et le sport, c'est qu'aucune défaite n'est mortelle, même en compétition : es-tu d'accord?

**Après avoir réfléchi
à ces questions
sur le fait de perdre,
tu peux en parler
avec tes parents ou tes amis.**

Dans la même collection

Application Max et Lili disponible sur

 App Store

Google play

 Suivez notre actualité sur Facebook
https://www.facebook.com/MaxEtLili